Text copyright © 1988 Shirley Isherwood
Illustrations copyright © 1988 Jill Bennett

First published in Great Britain in 1988
by Macdonald & Co (Publishers) Ltd

Reprinted in 1992 and 1994 by Simon & Schuster Young Books

Photoset in 18pt Bembo by Keene Graphics Ltd, London
Colour origination by Scantrans Pte Ltd, Singapore

Printed and bound in Belgium
by Proost International Book Production

Simon & Schuster Young Books
Campus 400
Maylands Avenue
Hemel Hempstead HP2 7EZ

BRITISH LIBRARY CATALOGUING IN PUBLICATION DATA
Isherwood, Shirley
William's problems.
I. Title
  823'.914[J]

ISBN 0-356-13950-6
ISBN 0-7500-0929-2 Pbk

William's Problems

Shirley Isherwood

Illustrated by Jill Bennett

SIMON & SCHUSTER
YOUNG BOOKS

Chapter One

William Barnes had problems.
Problem number one was that he
couldn't always get his b's and d's
the right way round.

^bdoy ^dboll

Problem number two was that his father had gone to work away from home, and William missed him. But that wasn't such a bad problem, because he'd soon be coming back.

William and his mother talked about him a lot, and about how wonderful it would be when he came home. It made them feel much happier.

They told William's little brother Matthew about how wonderful it would be. But Matthew was only one year old, and didn't seem to care one way or another. He just smiled and waved his rattle. When you are only one you don't have many problems, thought William. William was seven.

But problem number three was the biggest problem of all. William's grandfather was coming to live with them, and William would have to give up his nice big bedroom, so that Grandfather could move into it.

It was a wonderful room, and William loved it. It was big enough

for him to be able to set out his
model railway, and still have
enough space to leave all his other
toys lying about. William's habit of
leaving his toys lying about was a
problem, said his mother.

But William didn't think it was a
problem – it was just handy.

The day came when Grandfather and his furniture would arrive. William and his mother sat in the kitchen.

It was the last time that they would have breakfast alone.

As he ate his breakfast, William thought about his grandfather. He hadn't met him very many times

because Grandfather lived a long
way off, right at the other end of the
country.

But now he was coming to live in
William's bedroom.

"Why?" asked William.

"He's lonely," said William's
mother.

"Is being lonely a problem?" said
William.

"It can be," said his mother.

William went to school. In the middle of the morning his teacher asked everyone to write a story about an animal.

William thought that he would write a story about a bad dog, who went round digging in gardens, and barking at everyone.

Then he remembered the b's and d's. If he got them the wrong way round it might not say 'bad dog,' but 'dab bog' – which was silly.

So he wrote a story about a ginger cat instead.

It was quite boring.

Then he went home and found a
van standing outside the house.
Grandfather's furniture had arrived.

Chapter Two

William went to look at his old room. It was full of chests and a huge, old bed. The furniture almost filled the room.

"There will hardly be room for him to move about!" said William's mother.

"Why doesn't he get smaller furniture?" asked William.

"He's had these things a long time," said William's mother. "He's very fond of them. He doesn't want to give them up. It's a problem."

William went to look at his new room. It was very small and tidy – for there was no room to leave his things lying about.

William liked to see his things
lying about, and he understood how
Grandfather felt about his old chests
and his bed. But all the same he
grumbled about his new little room
all the way through tea.

After tea, Grandfather arrived. He
came from the station by taxi, and
he made the taxi driver sound the
horn, to let everyone know that he
was there.

Then he came stamping up the hall, and into the kitchen, and said "Hallo!" to everyone in a loud voice.

Every time he spoke his voice was loud. And he seemed to stare a lot, with his very blue eyes. He stared at William, and William's mother, and at Matthew and the cat.

"Does he always shout and stare at people?" asked William, when his mother tucked him into bed that night.

"Always," said his mother. "He's always been like that."

"Is it a problem?" asked William; for he wasn't sure if he liked his grandfather's way of shouting and staring.

"Not when you get used to it,"
said his mother.

William lay in bed, and wondered
if he'd ever get used to problems.

He wondered if he'd ever get used
to putting his things away neatly.

He wondered if he'd ever get used
to the problem of the b's and d's.

He wondered if he'd ever get used
to the new noises which came from
Grandfather's bedroom – the
twanging sound of the springs of the
bed and the sudden loud snores.

But the next evening, William found that they really did have a problem. Grandfather began to play his tuba in his bedroom. It made a big, deep noise, which filled the whole house. Then it began to play a low, rumpty-tumpty sort of tune.

William rather liked the music. It was the sort of noise, he thought, that a happy lion might make, if a lion could sing.

But the neighbours didn't like it.
Mrs Dart knocked on the wall. Mr
Humber came to William's house
and said that he couldn't hear his
television for the noise. The noise
also woke Matthew up, and he
began to cry.

"I don't know what we are going to do," said William's mother. "Grandfather loves playing his tuba. It will be really sad if he has to stop."

But Grandfather didn't stop playing the tuba. He just said "Rubbish!" when William's mother told him about the people next door.

"Everyone likes to hear a bit of music," he said. And he played every night – first the lion tune, and then a march, and then a very slow waltz, which made William think of big, black seals, walloping over in the water.

The neighbours kept complaining, and Matthew kept on waking up.

25

Then one night, between the lion tune and the march, William put a tape on his cassette player. The tape had been playing for a moment, when his grandfather knocked on the wall. William was very angry.

He went to his grandfather's room, where his grandfather sat on the edge of his bed, holding the tuba.

"*You* make a noise," said William. "Why can't I make a noise?"

"Children should be seen and not heard," said his grandfather.

William marched down the stairs and told his mother. "He said that children should be seen and not heard," he said. "What does that mean?"

"That's how children were meant to be when he was a little boy," said William's mother. "They were meant to sit quietly and not make a sound."

"Did he sit quietly?" asked William

"I don't suppose so," said his mother.

"Then why does he want me to do it?" said William.

"Oh, William!" said his mother. "Don't pester. I've got enough problems!"

Chapter Three

The next day was just as bad. At school, William got all his b's and d's the wrong way round.

His teacher tried to help him. "Draw the stick and then the circle to make a b," he said. "And draw the circle and then the stick to make a d."

But still William couldn't remember which way was which when he came to write the letters down.

"William Barnes is *stupid*," said a boy in William's class.

"No, I'm *not*," said William, and he went home in a bad temper, feeling very unhappy.

At home he found that Matthew was in a bad temper too, because

he was tired after being woken up in the night by Grandfather's tuba. He was crying, and William's mother was trying to soothe him.

She wasn't in a very good temper either, and she didn't seem to listen when William tried to tell her about the b's and d's going wrong, and about being called stupid. And it was all because of his grandfather, thought William.

William went out into the garden, and decided that everything was awful, and that he would run away from home. He ran off down the street, round the corner, and into the park.

But, once in the park, there didn't seem to be anywhere else to go. He went into the playground, but there was no one on the swings. Everyone was at home, having tea. William wandered round and round, feeling lonely, a bit frightened, and very hungry.

Then he began to run again – and as he went down the broad path, he saw his grandfather.

He was sitting on a bench, and when he saw William, he stuck out his walking stick, so suddenly that William almost fell over it.

"What are *you* doing here?" said William's grandfather.

"I'm running away!" said William.

"Why?" said his grandfather.

"I've got problems," said William.

"So have I," said his grandfather.

William was surprised. He had never thought of his grandfather having problems. He sat down on the bench and looked at him.

"What's your problem?" said William's grandfather.

William didn't like to say, "It's you!" So he said, "I can't get b's and d's the right way round."

"That's an easy problem to solve," said William's grandfather, and he took a notebook and a pencil from his pocket. "All you have to do," he said, "is draw a little bed, like this."

He drew a bed, with the stick of the b making the head of the bed, and the stick of the d making the foot. The circles of the letters made the middle of the bed.

Then he drew a little stick-man on the bed, with his head on the b and his feet on the d. Like this:

William took the notebook and the pencil and turned to a clean page.

Then he thought of the little bed, and made the b and d. They were the right way round, said his grandfather.

So William thought of other words with the letters b and d, and thought of the little bed and got the letters right. It was wonderful. One of his problems was solved.

Grandfather put away the notebook and they both got up and began to walk down the path.

William turned to look at his grandfather. "What's your problem?" he said.

"Living in someone else's house," said his grandfather. "That's my problem."

Chapter Four

William was more surprised than ever. William's problem was that his grandfather was living with him. And now his grandfather said that *his* problem was living with William.

They both had the same problem really, thought William.

"Don't you *like* living with us?" he asked.

"It's fine!" said his grandfather. "It just takes a little getting used to."

They turned round, and began to make their way back home for tea.

"Were you seen and not heard when you were a little boy?" said William, as they went.

"No," said his grandfather, "and I don't suppose that you will be – will you?"

"No," said William.

"Then I'll stop asking you," said his grandfather.

They went a little further, and then his grandfather spoke again.

"Sorry you got booted out of your room, William," he said.

"That's all right," said William. "I'll get used to it."

But there was still the problem of the tuba-playing. Everyone had a talk about it after tea – and it was William who solved the problem.

"Why don't you play in the morning?" he said. "Everyone's awake then, so the noise wouldn't matter."

"What a good idea!" said William's grandfather.

So they asked Mrs Dart and Mr Humber if they would mind if Grandfather played his tuba in the morning, and they both said, "Not at all!"

The next morning, before he went to school, William heard his grandfather play the lion song, and the walloping seal waltz. He whistled the tunes all the way to school.

In the afternoon his teacher asked everyone to write about someone they knew. William decided he would write about his grandfather.

'My grandfather has come to live with us,' he wrote. 'I didn't think I liked him at first. It gives you a bad feeling when someone lives with you, and you don't like them. But now I like him a lot better. I think he likes me. He still shouts when he talks, but my mother says he's always done that, so he isn't going to stop. He stares at you a lot, but I think that's just because he likes to have a good look at things.'

William's teacher liked what William had written. "It's very good, William," he said. "And you've got all your b's and d's the right way round. Well done!"

"No problem!" said William.

Other titles in the Storybooks series:

PRINTED IN BELGIUM BY

INTERNATIONAL BOOK PRODUCTION